THIS CANDLEWICK BOOK BELONGS TO:

____

____

____

First U.S. paperback edition 2011

The Library of Congress has cataloged the hardcover edition as follows:

Waring, Geoff.
Oscar and the snail : a book about things we use / Geoff Waring. — 1st U.S. ed.
p. cm.
Summary: When Oscar the kitten comes across a nest made of twigs and leaves, Snail explains why specific materials are chosen to do different jobs, where materials come from, and what useful qualities they have.
ISBN 978-0-7636-4039-2 (hardcover)
[1. Cats—Fiction. 2. Snails—Fiction. 3. Curiosity—Fiction.
4. Animals—Infancy—Fiction.] I. Title.
PZ7.W23530ss 2009
[E]—dc22 2009007352

ISBN 978-0-7636-5303-3 (paperback)

WKT 15 14 13 12 11 10
10 9 8 7 6 5 4 3 2 1

Printed in Shenzhen, Guangdong, China

This book was typeset in ITC Kabel.
The illustrations were created digitally.

Candlewick Press
99 Dover Street
Somerville, Massachusetts 02144

visit us at www.candlewick.com

CANDLEWICK PRESS

In memory of

Malcolm

The author and publisher would like to thank Sue Ellis at the Centre for Literacy in Primary Education and Martin Jenkins for their invaluable input and guidance during the making of this book.

OSCAR and the SNAIL

A BOOK ABOUT THINGS WE USE

Geoff Waring

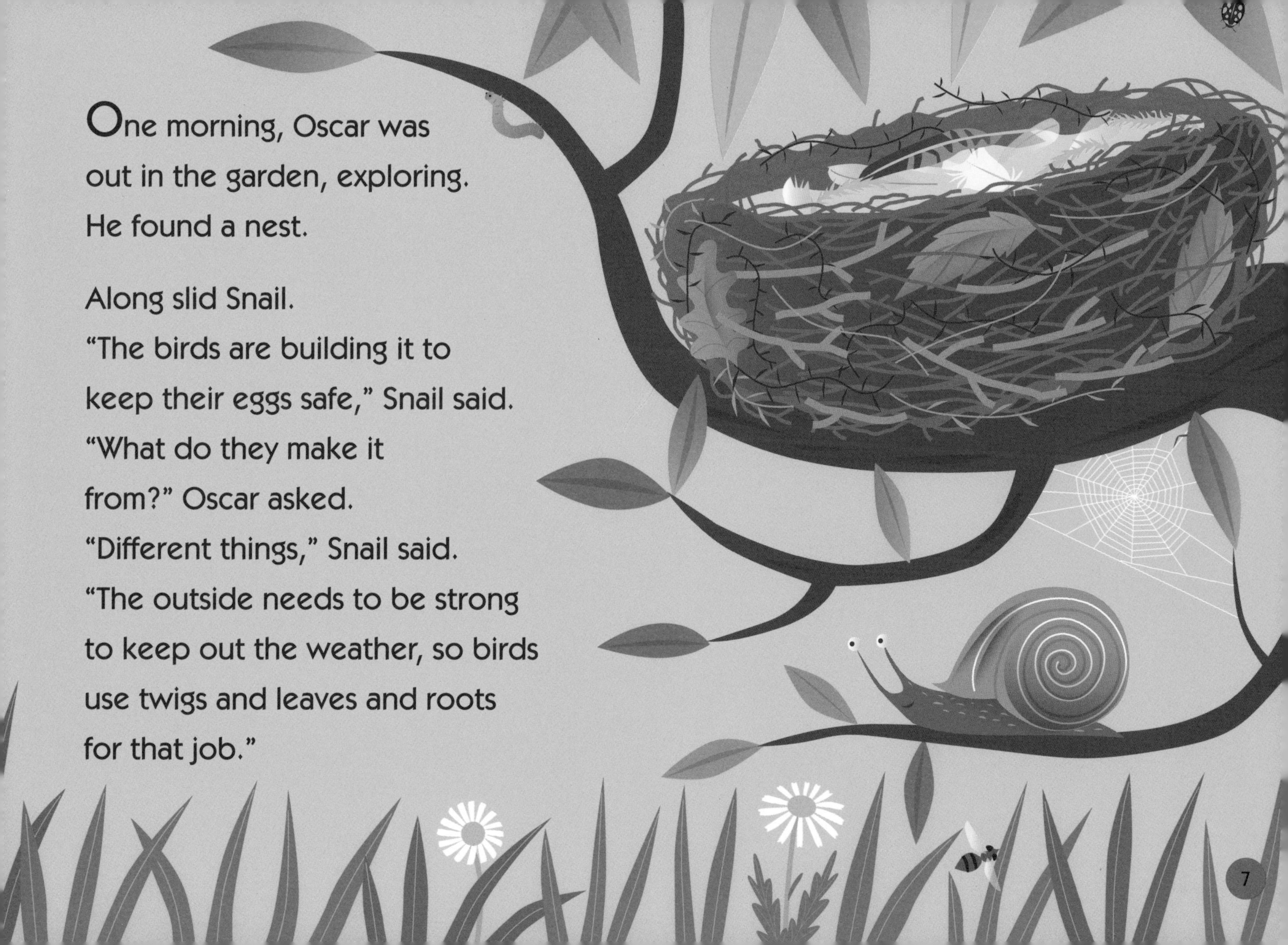

One morning, Oscar was out in the garden, exploring. He found a nest.

Along slid Snail.
"The birds are building it to keep their eggs safe," Snail said.
"What do they make it from?" Oscar asked.
"Different things," Snail said.
"The outside needs to be strong to keep out the weather, so birds use twigs and leaves and roots for that job."

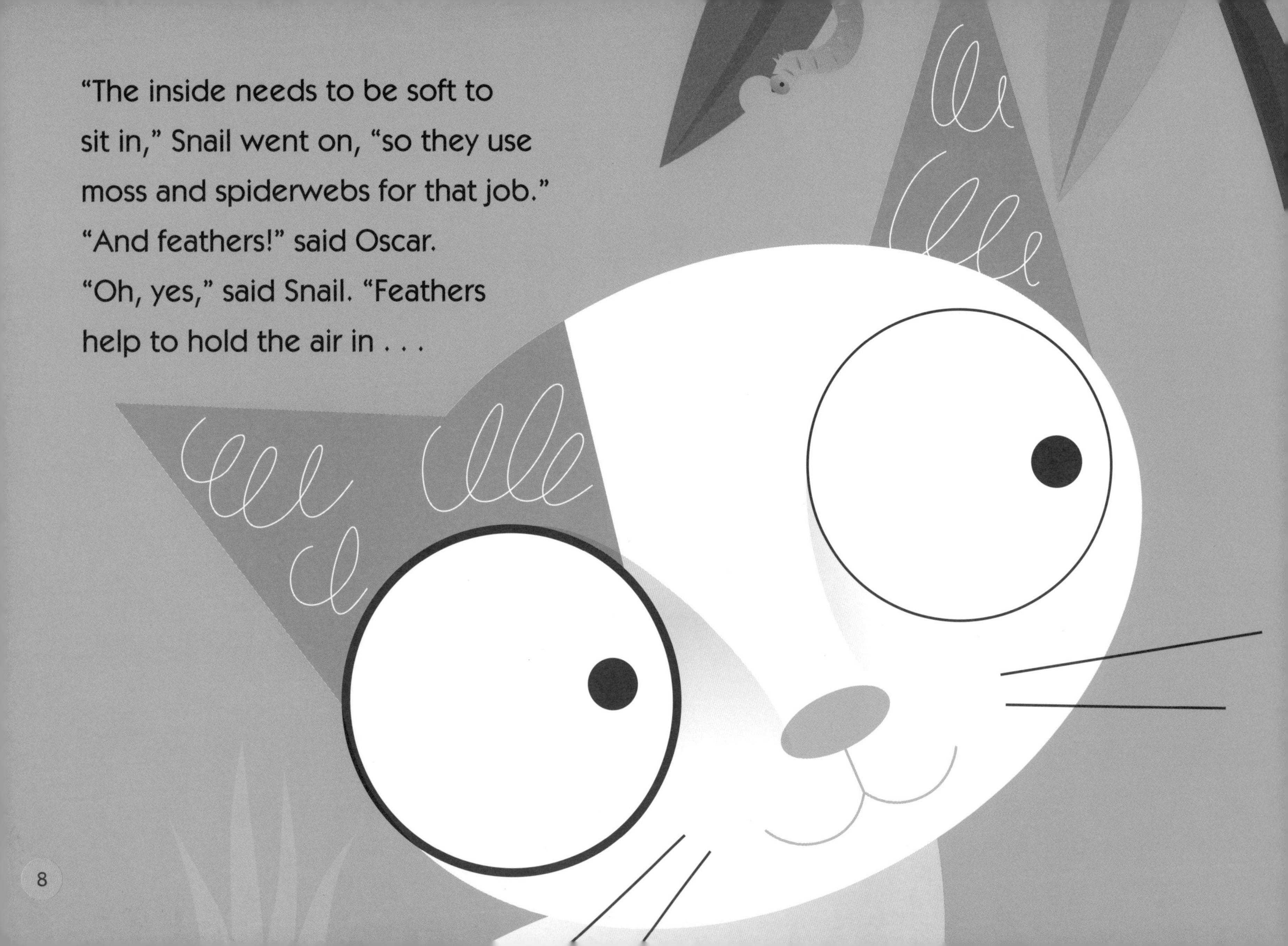

"The inside needs to be soft to sit in," Snail went on, "so they use moss and spiderwebs for that job."

"And feathers!" said Oscar.

"Oh, yes," said Snail. "Feathers help to hold the air in . . .

and keep the nest warm."

Just then, a loose
feather blew away . . .

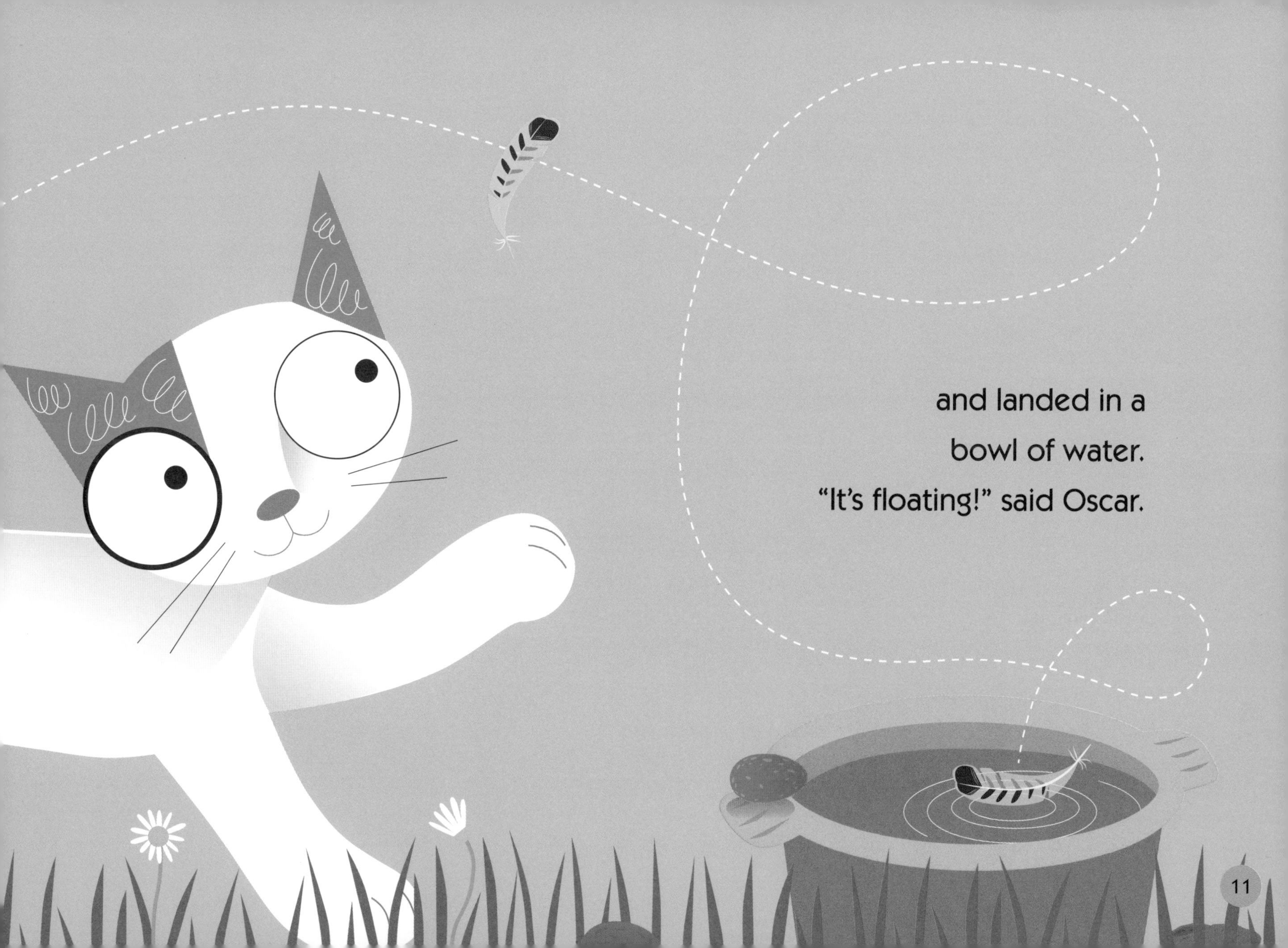

and landed in a
bowl of water.
"It's floating!" said Oscar.

Oscar pushed a stone into the bowl.

"Why isn't the stone floating?" he asked.

"Stones are heavy and don't have air in them, so they sink," Snail said. "A feather is light and has air inside, so it floats."

Oscar saw some more stones
in the vegetable patch.
"They're all different colors!" he said.
"Yes," said Snail. "They feel
different too. Some are rough and
some are smooth, but all of them
are heavy and useful for keeping
the netting weighed down."

It started to rain.

"Brrrrrr," Oscar said, shivering. "My fur's getting wet. I wish I had a shell like you."

"It's true," Snail said, "my shell does help keep me dry. But let's go to the greenhouse so that you can be dry and warm, too."

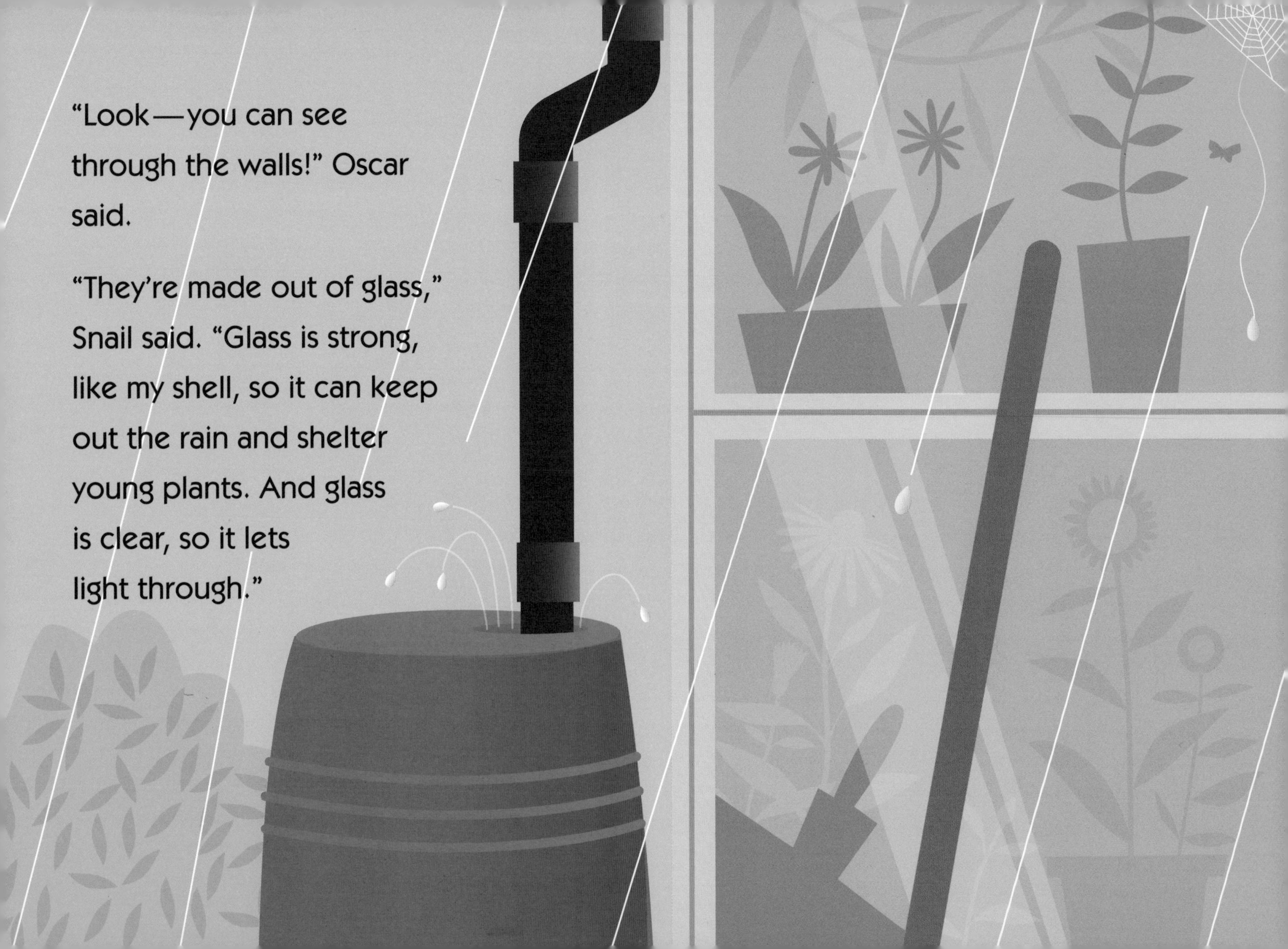

"Look—you can see through the walls!" Oscar said.

"They're made out of glass," Snail said. "Glass is strong, like my shell, so it can keep out the rain and shelter young plants. And glass is clear, so it lets light through."

“The sunlight warms the air inside the greenhouse,” Snail went on, “helping young plants grow.”

“Where does glass come from?”
Oscar asked.
“Glass is made out of sand,” Snail
said, “like the sand in this pile.

"If you make sand very hot, the grains melt together and become stretchy and clear. When it cools down, it sets hard and is glass."

Snail told Oscar about some other materials that are made.

Logs of wood are broken into tiny pieces, then squashed and rolled flat again and again to make paper.

When oil from deep underground is heated, it makes chemicals that can be mixed together to make plastic.

Seeds of wheat are ground into flour, then mixed with water and yeast to be baked into bread.

Clay, sand, and water are mixed together and baked in a very hot oven to make bricks.

Wool from sheep can be combed and spun into yarn to make cloth.

Just then, Poppy put her head around the door. “It looks nice and dry in here,” she said.

"It's warm, too," Oscar said. "You see, greenhouses are made out of glass. . . ."

And he told her about all the useful things he'd found out that morning.

Thinking about things that we use

In the garden, Oscar found out about . . .

Choosing materials

Living creatures use different materials to do different jobs.

Twigs to keep out the weather

Moss that is soft to sit in

Can you guess what some of the things you use are made of?

Using one material

One material has several different qualities:

Find something nearby. Can you discover what its different qualities are?

Where materials come from

Some materials are found in the natural world . . .

Twigs

Stones

and some materials are made.

Glass

is made out of

sand.

On your next walk, look out for things
that are natural and things that are made.

Index

Look up the pages
to find out about
these "material" things:

clear 18, 23

dry 17, 26

floating 11, 13

heavy 13, 14

light (in weight) 13, 28

light (visible) 18, 21

made 22–25, 27, 28–29

shelter 18

sinking 13

soft 8, 28

strong 7, 18

use 7, 8, 28

warm 9, 17, 21, 27, 28

Oscar thinks the things that we use are great! Do you think so, too?

Geoff Waring studied graphics in college and worked as an art director of *British Vogue*. He is currently creative director of *Glamour* magazine. He is the illustrator of *Black Meets White* by Justine Fontes. He says that the Oscar books are based on his own cat, Oskar. Geoff Waring lives in London.